Singles Retreat

A romantic novella
by Julia O. Greene

This is a work of fiction. All the characters and events portrayed in this novella are either fictitious or are used fictitiously.

Singles Retreat
by Julia O. Green
https://JuliaOGreene.com

Edited by Owl Pro Editing
https://owlproediting.com/

Book cover and interior design by Susan Stradiotto.
https://susanstradiotto.com

Printed in the United States of America

First Printing, 2019

Paperback ISBN-13: 978-1-949357-13-4
eBook ISBN-13: 978-1-949357-12-7

For my single girlfriends

who have waited so long to find that one love . . .

Julia

Capri Town

*I*taly has always been a dream. I imagined arriving in the romantic country with a partner, someone with whom I could share the experience. That part didn't come true, but this morning I stood on a small terrace overlooking the Sea of Capri and spent my first full day in the Mediterranean. These circumstances aren't—no, this retreat isn't—how I expected to visit. But, after raising two beautiful daughters and releasing them into the world, I am alone and have grown determined to chase my dreams one way or another.

It's time to make my way to the gardens for the retreat's welcome reception. Along the way, I stop for a shaved ice with Limoncello. As I wait in line at *Chiosco Tizzano*, the gelato stand, I try to hide that I am watching the people pass. The ones who seem alone and glance around nervously are most likely destined for the same reception as I. We'll meet soon in *Giardini di Augusto*, the botanical gardens, a handful of people desperate for companionship.

I try to think about the history of this island or really anything to distract myself. Capri just off the Amalfi Coast is where Roman royalty vacationed in villas with some regularity. It is said that Tiberius moved here when he grew weary of the politics in Rome and possibly feared assassination. It's quite a coincidence that this feared fate likely came to pass at the hands of Caligula.

In this perfumed place, truly the paradise that *Love Abroad*, the company sponsoring this retreat, advertises, I spent the morning relaxing and the afternoon wandering alone through the stone streets brightened by pink bougainvillea. What I'd really been trying to do was convince myself that I was doing the right thing...

1

that I wasn't crazy for coming halfway around the world to meet a man. Yes, I have talked with him for months via chat, email, and on the phone, and we even FaceTime regularly, but I've never met him in person. Jaxon. I sigh. I didn't even tell my girlfriends that I'd booked this trip. Only Iris knows how to find me, and I swore my youngest daughter to secrecy.

Turning back now is out of the question. If we meet and the chemistry isn't there, we'll be in the middle of a singles retreat. Chances are there will be plenty of others to meet. I step up to the counter and order. The Limoncello should round the edges of my anxiety—I hope.

Giardini di Augusto

$\mathscr{L}$auren, the event planner from Love Abroad, greets me, then shuffles through a box. "Ah, yes, Ren Hawkins. Here is your nametag. Please, take a glass of wine and have a seat in that section."

Accepting the lanyard, I turn to where the host points and take the farthest of the empty seats. There are only about twenty, which is nice. I'm early. Sometimes, I believe that's a bad habit, but I've always been that way. I still have my Limoncello. The wine can wait.

People trickle in but none that look familiar. I'm looking for his wavy hair, intense brown eyes, and that stubbled, strong jawline. It's probably wrong to come to these things for a prearranged meeting. After all, Love Abroad plans the events to encourage singles to meet new people in an age of e-dating. By default, I think Jaxon and I have broken their precepts. I keep searching, barely breathing, and holding the cup of Limoncello ice as if it's my last lifeline.

As the chairs fill, it seems that they've arranged for the women to be in one cluster and the men in another. What a disappointment. I keep looking and waiting for him. Maybe I was foolish to dish out this much money and leave the security of my parka in the cold Minnesota winter in desperate hope. But I need someone... a companion, a lover, my person. Since Luca passed, I've given my life to raising my daughters, to showing them how to be strong without a man, to teaching them that they can do anything on their own. Isn't it time that someone takes care of me?

Some of these people are young—a decade my junior if not more. It's absurd to think that any of them would be interested in a woman in her mid-forties. I'm in good shape for my age, but some of these men probably still want children. That part of my life is done. Jaxon—though we'd only ever seen each other from the shoulders up because neither of us wanted to defile a relationship that hadn't really begun—understood my stance on that. And he'd agreed. He also said he'd never wanted children of his own; and also in his mid-forties, he believed it was too late to start. So I had nothing to worry over. Except now, there was the niggling thought that he wouldn't come, that it was too good to be true, that I was one of those internet dating suckers who had fallen for the scam. Would it be wrong to ask the host if his name was on the list?

Probably. I wait.

The ice has nearly melted in the heat so I take a puckering sip, but before I can swallow, he saunters through the arched stone gate and our eyes meet. If magic existed, electricity would flow through thin air between us. My heart starts pounding as a grin spreads across his face. I swallow and smile back. I can't believe this is the first time we'll come face to face; I already know him so well. But then, with the sudden proximity, I wonder... how does he smell?

Please Mingle

$\mathcal{L}$auren, our host from Love Abroad, steps to the space in front of the small crowd and welcomes us all to Capri. As she gives her spiel, Jaxon and I sneak surreptitious glances across the aisle.

"I want to remind you of the rules you agreed to for this retreat," Lauren goes on. "We have these to ensure that you are getting adequate mingle time and aren't rushing into a fling that'll end as soon as the week is over. Please don't pair off immediately. We have group events planned for the first three days. If at the end of that you've gravitated toward that special someone, you are encouraged to conduct individual dates."

I try not to snicker at our—Jaxon's and my—plans, clearly a violation of those terms. Although, we'd discussed just this. We had concluded that it seemed like a safe way for us to get to know one another in person, with forced restrictions and in a group setting. I've been off the dating scene too long and haven't had sex with anyone since my husband died far too young from a car bomb in Iraq. This way, meeting didn't feel threatening. But I want...oh, how I want. Were there even others here now? I couldn't recall.

"...the most important rule here is to have a fabulous time," Lauren concludes.

The group claps, and I join in with little energy for the ovation.

After the applause, she redirects our attention to the tables behind us. "There are a buffet and beverages in the alcove down that path. Help yourselves. And please, mingle."

As a group, we all stand and start toward the flower-lined path. Introductions begin, but everyone except Jaxon is out of focus for me, blurry. One girl, while wringing her hands, introduces herself. Claire, I believe she says is her name. *Focus, Ren*, I encourage myself.

She's cute and thin. I take care of myself and am in pretty good shape, but I've never been thin. I hope thin isn't what Jaxon wants. Claire is probably five years younger than me, and her eyebrows shift nervously. If we were in any other situation, we'd probably be instant girlfriends. She sips her red wine and we make a bit of small talk on our way to the path. Again, I snatch a glance at him. He's performing the same routine with a sandy-haired man about his same size. Maybe I could...

"Should we go mingle with those two?" I nod toward Jaxon, asking Claire.

Dinner

It seems an eternity before we move toward one another, at last giving in to the magnetism that cloys in the air almost as thickly as the scent of freesia. He comes toward me, casual but seemingly reserved, as if he's nervous too. The thought makes me smile. I'm physically drawn to all of him—the way his light khaki pants hug his legs and the white shirt opens just enough to glimpse his well-formed chest, the way he walks with a hand in one pocket, the uncertain but hopeful half smile on his kissable lips, his dark eyes and matching hair and beard with just a hint of gray, and the one wave of hair that breaks loose and brushes his brow. In person, he's everything I had hoped for.

Be confident, comes my mental reminder as I walk over, trying with every ounce of strength to not check how my dress hangs or if my necklace is in the right place. When his smile breaks wider, I give in to my nerves and reach up with one hand to tuck a lock of my hair behind one ear. We naturally come face to face. He's only a hair's breadth taller than me, so we look one another in the eyes. My breath hitches.

"Good evening," comes his familiar voice. This time, it's not muffled by a poor connection. It's warm and heavy and smooth, like a blanket enfolding me and protecting me from the cold. I melt as he extends his hand. "Jaxon."

Eager, I place my hand in his. "Ren." The introductions are a game, but for the moment, it is only us.

Vaguely, I hear the other two introduce themselves, but they're not important. What's important is the lingering handshake and the tingle running up my arm. I'm shy and all the more awkward for the game. I don't want to let go. This feeling, this incredible spark between us, is exactly what I'd hoped for.

Someone clears their throat.

Claire whispers to the sandy-haired man, "I think this may be what love at first sight looks like."

I want to hold on, to pull him out of the garden with me, to blow the guise, but I don't. I release Jaxon's hand and put on a mask of politeness as I break eye contact. Claire and Jaxon introduce themselves and I meet Don. There's nothing, no feelings of excitement or anticipation, when I shake his hand.

"Shall we eat?" asks Don.

I'd forgotten about food. Had I been hungry? There was only one thing I hungered for in the moment, but that had to be saved. The anticipation was already enough. How would it be after three more days of in-person courtship? Or… after three days of playing at this singles game, speed dating almost.

When we finish our meals, a small bell rings and Lauren steps to the center of the smattering of four-person tables. "Now, mix it up. Give yourselves the opportunity to meet everyone."

My stomach suddenly feels like it will heave.

The Dance

*M*agnetic is the only way to describe it. I meet several other people, but their names don't stick as I keep getting distracted by Jaxon and the other women he's meeting. It's painful to watch, and it occurs to me how unfair it is to these men, what I'm doing. Is it unfair to those women too?

A quartet arrives as we're mixing and meeting each other. Lauren encourages people to dance.

"Ren?" the man I'm dancing with calls. What was his name?

I make a noise, one intending to acknowledge him. It's a lousy attempt, and I'm well aware of that. The bell rings again, and he doesn't look disappointed to leave me for the next woman in line. The thought of speed dating runs through my mind again. I'm alone for a moment, searching for Jaxon, when I feel a soft touch on my shoulder.

When I turn, he opens his arms. I move into his embrace, a place I've longed to be for months now. And we fit. We stand still with our noses almost touching, neither speaking and our breath mingling. I inhale, feeling his scent permeate every fiber of my body. Amber and caramelized vanilla—rich, earthy, and more intoxicating than wine.

He pulls me closer and begins to move. We fit this way, too, and I muse about how else we'll fit. I follow his movement, giving him the control to lead me where he will.

"I've been waiting to have you in my arms since I walked through that gate," he says.

"Truly?"

"Mmhmm . . . I think we worried over a lack of chemistry for nothing."

"I think it's physics. Magnetism comes to mind." As soon as the words are out, I want to palm my face. My nerd shows. I look down, face heating.

He lifts my chin. "Something so enjoyable about you, how you always reach for an analogy that's true, but unlike what everyone else says." He runs a hand over my warm cheek.

We dance quietly for several minutes until the song stops. Everyone applauds the quartet, and as they take up a new song, Jaxon and I take a seat at one of the tables—another broken rule. There are no questions between us like what's our favorite movie or book, none about family, and nothing about what we do for work. Those topics have already been covered through FaceTime. They were safe topics as we'd both agreed that intimacy would be awkward through the internet—even though that's how we met. With the beauty of this island, that minutia is impossible to think about anyway.

Leaning in, he asks, "Should we have just met one-on-one?"

"No," I lie. "This is good. We didn't know if we'd be a match in person, right?"

"Right...," he says, arching one dark brow. "Don't you think it's going to be tough for you over the next few days? Look at all these single men you'll be fighting off."

Grotta Azzurra

The following morning, I awoke to birds chirping outside the open window and a cool breeze billowing through the curtains. I push my hair out of my eyes and start toward the bath. Something at the door catches my eye, but it can wait. Necessities call. When I return, I realize it's an envelope. I open the flap and read.

> Ren,
>> *I'm counting the hours until they allow us away from the group activities. Until then, I'll play the game.*
>>> In anticipation,
>>> Jaxon

I'm standing there with an amused grin, happier than I could imagine over a simple two-line note and remembering his hand about my waist as we danced and the way I trembled when he touched my arm.

Rap, rap, rap. The knock startles me from the daydream. I jump, pull my robe tighter and crack the door, hoping absurdly that it's Jaxon. But it's only Lauren, here to share the plans for the day—a day cruise around Capri and Anacapri.

I dress and go to the terrace where the group gathers. Everyone gets a questionnaire to complete over breakfast. Apparently, there's another activity, a scavenger hunt of sorts, in which we are to match an answer with a specific person. I sit with Jaxon and we make a game of our own over the questions. Again, it strikes me how unfair it is that we can each already fill out the other's. The scavenger hunt is tomorrow; it could be fun.

After breakfast, we agree to try to adhere to the retreat rules and keep our distance. Before he boards the first gondola, he whispers, "In anticipation."

I echo and wait for the second car down to the pier where we board a boat just large enough to hold everyone. By the time I board, Jaxon is already in the bow with others sitting close. A tiny woman with full blonde curls sits beside him. I find my way to the back and take a seat, hopeful that she's not the type he desires physically.

Don sits next to me, and we strike up a conversation. He's nice, platonically nice. Claire sits on my other side and the three of us laugh over small talk as the boat leaves the dock. I'm curious why they have me sandwiched between them as they flirt with one another across my lap. I look for Jaxon's eyes, and as if he feels the connection turns away from the woman beside him. He doesn't even try to hide it as he looks my way. She follows his gaze, and I return to my conversation with a small smile.

The captain speaks to Lauren in Italian, beautifully lilting, and I wish I could understand. That's something I have never asked Jaxon—if he can speak Italian. His last name, Andolini is most certainly of Italian origin. Our host from Love Abroad turns on the microphone and translates for us, outlining the agenda. When she's finished, the boat's captain turns on some night-club danceable music while Lauren pours and passes around some sparkling wine.

Lauren continues to act as our guide, narrating the sights as we sail. "There is *Salto di Tiberio*, Tiberius's Leap in English, where it is rumored that the emperor had disloyal servants tossed to their deaths." "That is the home of Curzio Malaparte, *Casa Come Me*. If you have interest in political history, he had quite the love-hate relationship with the Fascist Party and Mussolini." "And ahead, we'll pass under the famed stone arch in the smallest of the Faraglioni rock formations—Faraglione di Mezzo. If you're so inclined for a romantic luncheon, you can make a reservation there at *La Fontalina* and swim at the quiet, rocky beach afterward. *Molto romantico!*"

When I feel Jaxon turn to look at me, I nod once in silent agreement. Apparently, even with the adorable little lady beside him, his mind is still with me. I get fluttery just thinking about it.

We continue on, the boat passing the little marina and visiting two grottoes that capture the most vibrant blues and greens, then the lighthouse. We travel along the northern coast, spotting goats climbing the rock face before we stop so that we can enter the Grotta Azzurra in small row boats. Four to a boat, Jaxon and I linger so that we can be together on the last one loaded. He sits in the back, I just in front of him. When the boat approaches the entry, the skipper tells us to sink down as low as possible, and I settle back onto Jaxon's chest.

When we enter the cave, he reaches up and brushes his fingers on the rock. It's cool inside, much cooler than it's been in the sun all day, and the blue glow takes my breath away. There are several other boats inside, and the skippers all join in an Italian serenade that echoes around the cavern.

Jaxon dips his head and whispers the words, the Italian words, to the song in my ear. I guess that answers my question from before. His breath is hot on my neck, and when there's a break in the serenade, he inhales and says, "I want you." He kisses his way up my neck to my ear.

I feel it in my stomach, lower, and all the way to my toes, and I fight the moan that threatens to escape. "Two more days?"

"If we must."

I turn to face him, afraid to let our lips touch so as to not ignite anything more.

"Okay," interrupts the skipper, "here we go."

As soon as he says this, we're under the arch again. I jump when the water splashes against the rock and sprays us inside the boat. It's as if nature is telling us to wait just a little longer.

Mount Solaro

By the second morning, I awaken sexually frustrated and need to take care of myself before I can join the others for the day. The sun is peeking brightly through my window. I close my eyes and remember Jaxon's strong arm around my waist while dancing in the Piazzetta and the tickle of his soft kisses on my neck and shoulder while we were in the shadows at the Blue Grotto. I recall his breathy words, *I want you*, and I'm ready, on the edge before I even touch myself. The whole thing is quick, probably less than a minute, but the flood of release eases my need . . . a little.

After, I shower, dress in hiking clothes, and toss a small backpack over my shoulder for the day. Our activity for today is hiking Mount Solaro. At breakfast, we're each given a list of facts about random people in the group. Our job is to put names to the tidbits of information. I scan the list and find, *He enjoys spending time alone in his tiny cottage on a private island in northern Maine.* I grin and in the blank under the random fact, I write *Jaxon Andolini*.

As soon as I've written it, my chest tightens with anxiety. We haven't talked about the distance. If we take a step into intimacy, how will our relationship grow when we're separated by more than a thousand miles? I remember Luca—yes, I have a thing for Italian men—and the times we were reunited after he'd been deployed. When he came home, we always spent days reacquainting ourselves with each other. That was before the girls, and the lovemaking had been devastatingly passionate.

Stop that Ren! I tell myself. Luca has no place here. Yet I can't help but wonder if my late husband would approve. I think he would want me to be happy, but it's hard to be certain as we'd never had that particular conversation. Though the passion I once shared

15

with Luca after our separations gives me hope that the same could be true in a relationship where we each live in different places. Heaven knows I'm not moving away from my girls or my mother back in the Cities. I don't know if he'd be willing to move to the Midwest, but I fear pushing him away by asking. That is a conversation for the future. For now, I'll assume we can both travel from time to time. Besides the money from the insurance, I do well in my marketing career.

We take two buses to *Piazza della Pace* in Anacapri. They're smaller than normal tour buses, so half of us ride in one while the others follow in a second. Jaxon and I are separated— intentionally—once again. It's day two. Thankfully we're getting closer to being released to our own agendas. I'm thankful for the physical activity on today's itinerary. It should be a distraction.

At the Piazza, some choose to ride up on the chairlift. Both Jaxon and I embrace the opportunity for the hike. It's rumored to be steep but should only take about an hour. A few others tackle the climb as well, Claire and Don included. Jaxon allows me to go first and follows. I'm breathing hard when we reach the top and the most beautiful sights I have ever seen come into view—an expansive view of the entire island, the rock formations surrounding Capri, and the deepest blue Mediterranean Sea stretching to the horizon in one direction and to Sorrento in the other. Overwhelmed by the magical view, I turn into Jaxon's arms, and he welcomes me with a grin that says he's as anxious as I for the organized part of this retreat to be over.

"Not yet, lovers," Lauren calls from across the summit.

We separate, chagrined if no longer shy of one another.

Da Antonio, Anacapri

After some time to explore the apex of Mount Solaro, we hike down to the hermitage of *Centrella*, a small and quaint church, and then onward to a snack bar near the lighthouse, *Da Antonio*, which serves nice drinks and small plates. Jaxon and I grab two sun loungers and stretch out to catch the rays of the lowering sun. Lauren comes around to collect our answers to the scavenger hunt. I hand her my list first, not unfolding it to show that I've only collected three names including Jaxon's. He unfolds his, and to my delight, there is only one name on his paper. Lauren gives us both a scolding look and moves on to the others nearby. I look at Jaxon, and we both break out in laughter. I'm wiping away a tear and holding my gut before the fit subsides.

"In all honesty, what harm is there that we are already decided?" Jaxon asks.

I thought for a moment. "None, I suppose. But that little lady with the blonde hair sure had her eye on you. Don't you think we're being rude?"

"Not my type." Jaxon turns sideways in his chair to face me. "I think it would be more rude to pretend I'm interested in someone I am not."

I turn to him, our knees interlocking. "Touché. We have another day, though, and I want to visit the ruins of *Villa Jovis*."

"Mmhmm. Villa of Jupiter. You do know that we don't have to remain with this group to do that," he says.

"It's included in the retreat." As I say this, we're moving closer and closer together.

He nods simply and touches my arm. Electricity zings up my arm from the contact.

Lauren clears her throat disapprovingly as she passes us. "Gather around. Let's announce the winners of the scavenger hunt."

Our foreheads rest together for a moment, but we stand and join the others. I'm a queen at self-denial after so many years of choosing to be alone, so I tell him, "I think we can make it through tomorrow."

Lauren reads off a few of her favorite facts then announces the winners. No surprise, neither of our names are called. But as we stand there, he takes my hand and I feel like a teen on her first date. In some ways, I am.

People rave about beach sunsets, but they hold no comparison to the view from the deck of Da Antonio to the west over the Mediterranean. We watch the sun turn into a ball of fire over the water—in all honesty, the most brilliant sunset I've ever seen. That Jaxon wraps his arms around me just as the bottom of the fiery ball touches the water makes me believe it might be the best one I will ever see.

Villa Jovis and Da Luigi

After hiking the ruins of Villa Jovis, we return to *Marina Piccola* and take shuttle boats to the restaurant overlooking the giant standing rocks, *Da Luigi ai Faraglioni*. It's the end of the third day now, so Jaxon and I find a quiet table for two along the railing overlooking the sea. Lauren has given up on keeping us apart, and we've become tagalongs with the group rather than participants.

With glasses of white wine in hand, we await our main meal, the fresh catch of the day. The waiter assures us the white fish with lemon will melt in our mouths.

Jaxon raises a glass. "To first meetings."

"To our time in Capri."

We clink glasses, but before he takes a sip he adds, "And all the times to follow."

The wine is refreshing with hints of crisp citrus. What better taste for a place famous for lemons the size of cantaloupes? I lean toward the handsome man before me. "I'm going to be sore from all the hiking."

"We'll do something more relaxing tomorrow," he says with a glint in his eye.

I narrow my eyes. "You're planning something already."

He drinks again without a word.

"Well, thank you for agreeing to stay for the tour of Villa Jovis today. I'm in love with Roman history. Learning about Tiberius, his short temper, and his rumored debauchery were absolutely fascinating."

"Can you imagine what he'd face if he pulled those stunts today?"

We share more laughter as the skies darken into a blue as deep as the sea. The sound of water crashing and soft music from inside set a lovely atmosphere. Driven by desire, I throw caution to the breeze over the sea. "I no longer think she'd notice if you came to my room this evening."

Jaxon raises a perfect brow and cocks a half grin. "You don't think she would?"

I shake my head and paint a devious smile across my lips. I have put off my needs for so long, tried to quell this yearning, been a good mother for Lily and Iris. I am tired. Selfish though it may be, I want this man in my bed. Tonight.

Jaxon reaches forward and takes both my hands. "I want nothing more than to spend a long and luxurious night getting to know every inch of your body."

Oh no. My stomach sinks. I feel a *but* coming. I hold my breath.

He kisses my knuckles. "You've already said that you need rest from the hiking. For what I have in mind, you will need every last drop of energy you can muster."

My mouth goes dust dry. "Really?" I choke out.

He sips the wine. "Mmhmm."

The waiter brings our dinner. I should thank him, but I can't tear my eyes from Jaxon, let alone catch enough breath to voice the words.

Buona Notte

*W*e're holding hands as he walks me to my door. We haven't kissed yet, and I want so much more. I don't care how exhausted my body is, there is a sexual energy flooding throughout my bloodstream. I'm uncomfortably damp and absolutely on fire with white-hot desire.

"This is me." I stop and slide a key into the door to open it.

Jaxon grabs my wrist and with a swift tug, I'm nestled in his arms. His hand reaches up my neck and under my hair. He looks in my eyes with his intense brown stare and lets it fall to my lips. The first kiss is gentle, barely a kiss at all. The second is soul-crushing, an explosion of all the tension we've built up over the last three days. Our tongues dance more sensually than any tango. Our breathing becomes raspy. He bites my lower lip and trails kisses down my neck.

I groan in frustration. "Let me ope—"

He cuts off my words with another searing kiss, only to break it a second later and stare through my eyes and into my very being. I need this man like water. It's like I've been starving for twenty years and he is a seven-course meal spread before me. He places his finger on my lips and molds his body to mine. I feel the bulge in his pants… so close to home if it weren't for the accursed clothes separating us.

"Make no mistake, Ren." He moves against me. "I crave this as much as you. But I will do this right, and tonight is only almost right." He kisses me deeply again. "*Bellisima! A domani. Buona notte, mia cara.*" And he walks away, leaving me in desperate need.

Sorrento

I wake up sweating, but not in the way that I'd hoped the evening before. It's dark outside. The birds aren't singing yet, and I'm trying to bury the visions I just worked through in my dream state. *It's not real,* I tell myself. The truth is only part of it's real, but it's all a jumble. Scenes from my marriage to Luca intermingled with scenes from now with Jaxon. They crossed and became confused. Jaxon was the one who returned from overseas and we romped in our bedroom for hours until one of us got hungry enough to get up. The scene switched and Luca spoke Jaxon's words sent through FaceTime, *My history with women hasn't been a good one.*

I sit half-covered, running my fingers through tangled hair, and try to sort the pieces back into the piles where they belong. Luca was my military man, happy and charismatic. He never had trouble with women, even back to high school. But somehow, I was the girl who won him. I wipe away a tear; that particular crack in my heart would never fully mend. The joy of those reunion scenes belonged—no, still belong—to him.

Jaxon is the one leery of relationships. I can't understand how a mother could do such a thing, but she abandoned him and his father when he was six. He's a beautiful man, but being raised by a different woman every year of his life since then did some lasting damage. In college, he did what was expected—dated and partied and courted many young women—until he ended up in some legal drama when one accused him of assault. As it turned out, he wasn't even at the party. He's part of society in New York, that much he inherited from his father. He's even been named the most eligible bachelor in the city. But he said he didn't want the same string of women his father had and that being close to them physically didn't allow him to truly connect with anyone. He's told me all these stories over our near year of online conversation. God, I feel like I know him so well in so many ways except one.

I can't believe this feeling that's blooming, but is it possible to be in love even though it was only yesterday that we shared our first kiss? Maybe it counts differently when you've been talking for so long. I don't really know. I'm confused and supercharged on desire. But then again, how will we be after we're together, and after we return to our separate lives?

Stop worrying, my girlfriends always tell me. Hell, my girls have taken up the mantra lately.

I throw off the covers and go out onto the terrace. Even from this high in the center of the island, in the early morning, I hear the waves crashing against the rocks. There's little other sound in paradise when only a sliver of light breaks on the horizon. I stand there for a long time and watch the sun's rays shoot into the sky and a star of light grow in the distance until it's a half ball of fire. It's a new day.

I dress and center myself. When I open my door, Jaxon is leaning against the wall, waiting for me. My heart does a little pitter-patter and I melt at his smile.

"Did you sleep well?"

I wish I could say yes, but I just shrug.

He nods. "I hope that's not my fault."

I shake my head. "No. It's my muddled brain trying to work out the past and future."

He knits his brows together, then raises one in question.

"Never mind. Should we have breakfast?" I ask.

He stands and opens his arms to me, and I gravitate toward him. He gives me a gentle kiss on the forehead and says, "Sure. And after, you can pack."

Pushing away, startled, I ask, "Pack?"

"Mmhmm."

"I have the room for five more days."

"I've taken care of that." He urges me toward the stairs. As we walk, he adds, "I've also arranged for a boat to take us to Sorrento."

"But the hotel said it was nonrefundable."

"They've only charged you for the days you stayed. Check your account. I told them I'd pay for the rest."

Oh is all I can say for a long moment. My thoughts are jumbled. I've never had anyone arrange vacations for me. Hell, when I was married, we were too young and broke to go on vacations, which then only consisted of a weekend sequestered in a cabin in the Northwoods of Minnesota—something inexpensive. And that was only before our sweet Lily arrived. We walk down the stairs and to the open-air restaurant for breakfast. As we're sitting, I find my voice again. "What about a hotel in Sorrento?"

He opens the menu. "I have a villa."

My eyes pop wide open. "You own a villa? In Sorrento?" My voice carries and people turn to look at us. I warm under the attention. "Sorry," I say to the nearest table.

He laughs smoothly. "No, I rented one. But the point is that you don't need to worry about the logistics. We'll take our time getting there and spend the late afternoon relaxing by the pool before we venture out for dinner this evening."

It seems he has everything planned. We'd discussed that if everything went well, we'd spend the end of our trip together alone. He made some big assumptions in arranging everything, but I don't want to object. Inside, I feel all warm, light, and . . . happy.

Cala di Mitigliano

*L*auren congratulates us on our way from the hotel and snaps a photo. She promises not to use names, but we did sign a release that she could use our pictures to show how successful the Love Abroad retreats can be. I want to roll my eyes, but I smile sweetly and thank her as Jaxon pays for a porter to haul the luggage to the private boat awaiting our arrival in Marina Piccola.

On board, the captain greets us with two mimosas and shows us around his boat. It's on the smaller side but more than enough for the captain and the two of us. "We have lunch and waters packed in the cooler." He points. "And if you'd like more wine, I'll be your waiter. Otherwise, sit back and enjoy your day."

"Cala di Mitigliano?" Jaxon asks.

"Si, si," answers the captain as he turns on the radio.

"What is Cala de Mi—?" I ask.

"Mitigliano. A quaint little beach south of Sorrento sheltered by a little cove. Lunch and swimming."

We sit back, me cuddled up to Jaxon, and we turn our faces into the breeze. Once we're beyond the no-wake zone, the boat picks up speed. I grab my cap and loop my ponytail through the strap so the hat doesn't fly away.

Jaxon asks, "How are your girls?"

"They're fabulous. The weekend before I left, Lily's boyfriend asked me if he could propose to her while I was away." I remain quiet after that; the memory brings back the fact that her father isn't there.

Jaxon lifts my chin. "It must be hard for you to carry both parental roles."

"It's old hat." I giggle and shrug, attempting to dismiss the discomfort over Luca coming into this moment.

As if reading my mind, he says, "He still has a place in your life. I cannot *and don't want to* erase that."

I choke on my words. "Th-thank you. You're so amazing about that. The handful of losers I've dated since Iris went to college haven't been as understanding." I chuckle, nervous again. "You'd think after so long my grief wouldn't be so obvious."

"I'm sure a loss like that stamps your soul."

We share a knowing glance and hug each other tighter. I know he's thinking about his mother, and she has a place here, too, even if I don't know how to fix anything about that situation. It wasn't the same kind of loss, but it was a loss still. The silence between us is enough. It amazes me how comfortably we fit. We settle into one another and ride in silence to the beach.

When the captain pulls the boat to a stop, I look over the side through the clear blue water to the rocky bottom. The water when I enter is bath-like, and even far away from the shore where a small smattering of people frolic in the water, the bottom is within reach.

I'm only in for a few minutes before Jaxon grasps me and pulls me into him, holding me tight around the waist. I taste saltwater on his lips when ours meet and devour each other. The scratch of his beard against me is one of the most erotic feelings. I plunge my hands into his wet hair and gasp for breath in between searing kisses. I wrap my legs around his waist, feeling him grow within his swim shorts. The damn clothes are still in the way, and I mewl with frustration as I tilt my face to the sun and he kisses me behind my ear. Chills run up and down my entire body.

When I come back to face him, he says, "I love the length of your legs around me." He kisses me again and pulls my hips closer so that I feel how tight his erection really is and whispers, "Tonight—if I can wait."

Villa Lia

$\mathcal{A}$bout dinner time in Sorrento, everyone pours onto the streets for a social hour and stroll. Jaxon and I join in the tradition and make our way to a chic local restaurant with white-on-white décor called *Pepe Bianco*. The dining room is small and well lit, but it still feels delectably private. We make small talk for a while. He says his work in finance is going well, but some of his father's campaigners are trying to pull him into New York's politics—something he's dead set against. I don't have much to contribute to a conversation about my work. Work is work, but it keeps me busy. I focus more on the lights of my life, Lily and Iris.

The food and wine are amazing and light, not the heavy pizza and pasta that we stereotypically pin on the Napoli area in Italy. That food can be had, but it typically comes with tourists. Pepe Bianco caters to locals and, apparently, those with the inside track.

When we're done, we walk slowly over the cobbled roads and peruse the goods in many of the stores along the streets that lead into the heart of the area, *Piazza Tasso*. We touch each other as much as we can. The energy between us thrums in mutual anticipation. At one point, despite any people who may be milling around, our eyes lock and we kiss sweetly. With little urging, Jaxon has me up against a wall and presses his rock-hard body into mine. He seizes my mouth with a force that tells me he's tired of this foreplay.

When he sets me free, I breathe, "Should we return to Villa Lia?"

I don't need any more of an answer than the intensity of his dark eyes boring into mine. I rub my tingling bottom lip as we head to the villa. At the door, I brazenly kiss him, my hands tugging at his clothes, as he fumbles with the keys and opens the door. He turns from me for only a moment to toss the keys toward the table. They miss, but who cares? I've been waiting twenty years for this very night, and any of the men who'd seemed a potential candidate when I first started dating couldn't hope to live up to the sexiness of this man.

He turns to me ravenously, reaches for me, and lifts me against the wall. Like I'd done in the water earlier, I wrap my legs around his waist, and the full girth of him comes right to my core. Again, damn the clothes to hell. He rocks his hips as he trails wet kisses down my neck. We make dry love, only I am drenched. When he comes away, I'm certain I'll leave a wet spot on his pants, through both my panties and my linen pants.

Mutual need drives us single-mindedly forward, and we don't make it to the bedroom. We don't even make it to the couch. He places me on my feet only long enough to strip the clothes from my body, then from his. Before I know it, I'm backed up against the wall and blessedly exposed.

He's poised, ready to enter, and my core is throbbing for the sharp sensation I know is coming. Then he growls and lets his head fall backward.

I gasp. "What?"

"Protection?"

"The baby factory is closed."

"You're sure?"

I nod.

He kisses me, and moans into my mouth as he presses slowly inside. Once I've taken him all, he waits. We both adjust, sighing and enjoying the feel of finally knowing one another in this way too. We kiss for what seems another eternity until I begin whimpering, the need to move urging me onward. I try to squirm to get him to respond, but he holds me tighter against the wall.

He teases, "Is there something you want? Something I can do for you?"

I can barely find my voice. "Mm-hm-hm."

He moves slightly, and I make a noise that sounds dangerously like a moan of ecstasy.

"What was that?" He drops a kiss on my collarbone.

A shiver racks my spine. "Please," I beg.

"Yes?" he drawls.

Words are gone.

"Has the wait been worth it?" He moves a foot, steadying himself.

"Mmhmmm."

"And you want more?" He's perturbingly still. How the hell is he handling the building tension?

"Yes! Oh God! YES!"

"How much more?"

I mewl. "All"—*pant*—"of"—*pant*—"you"—*pant*...

"That's what I wanted to hear." He moves.

Just one move, and everything explodes. Stars—no, fireworks—go off behind my eyelids. My body locks down, and I hold on to his shoulders with everything I have as he drives into me faster, harder, faster. My orgasm won't release me as his builds as if it, too, waits for us to fall over the edge together. His breathing gets harder; he grunts and thrusts—hard, fast, punishing. My orgasm keeps roiling, and I cry out again and again so loudly that people on the beach might hear me. At last, he cries out, too, and his body freezes and twitches uncontrollably, his face buried in my shoulder as he breathes my name.

I'm floating...high. Then...I fall. We fall. Everything pulsates as I recover and he softens inside me.

The End

This morning, I woke glowing, and relished again our repeated lovemaking. Now, as I pack to return to Minnesota, sadness tugs at my heart. We've spent four more days enjoying one another, both in private and public. We fit in all ways now, except—no, I can't think like that. Last night, when I was on the edge of sleep, I think he whispered the words. Words I hadn't heard spoken to me since Luca. Words I wanted to whisper back except for the fact that I believe he believed I was sleeping. Words I am now afraid of in the daylight on our last morning in this beautiful place.

We move around one another like the other is already gone. It seems we're both fighting saying anything that will cast a shadow over the past few days. But the silence is killing me as much as the impending goodbye. *Stop it, Ren!* I tell myself. We are both privileged enough that we can see each other frequently, and as I've known all along, there isn't a chance I will be moving to New York. I look at him for a moment before I throw my last clothes in the bag, considering. Maybe I should ask if he'll ever consider moving to Minnesota. I decide against it. Maybe after we spend some more time together in person.

We finish packing and he carries the bags to the street to await the driver.

At the Napoli airport, we go to the same airline but different attendants. Our flights are less than two hours apart, his leaving before mine. I'll have time to cry once he's gone.

The lady at the counter says, "You're all set. Seat 2A."

Dropping my brows, I respond, "There must be some mistake, I didn't pay for first class."

She checks my passport and the computer again. "Ren Hawkins?"

I nod.

"There's no mistake. You're assigned to seat 2A. Enjoy your flight."

When I turn to Jaxon, he's smirking.

I backhand him playfully with my ticket. "You did this."

"It's the least I can do as a goodbye."

A solid lump forms in my throat that I have to swallow before I can speak. "Let's not say that word. Please."

We go to security and through the fast line as we're both scheduled to fly first class. I walk him to his gate. They're already boarding, so he puts down the bags and grabs me around the waist, pulling me close and kissing me hard... then soft. His kiss says everything that I feel, and I try to hold back the tears.

"I guess we can FaceTime tomorrow after we're both home." My words are awkward, quiet, and unsure.

He just nods and tells me to go on. "I'll talk to you soon."

At my gate, I do cry. In fact, I ugly cry, and I simply don't care who might see. I never anticipated this would be so hard. Everything was so perfect here, but now what? Just like the thoughts that had crossed my mind several times before—a long-distance relationship, which is less than ideal, comes to mind.

On the plane, I grab a glass of wine and stare out the window. Seat 2B is empty, and I hope it remains that way. The flight attendant brings me headphones and a heated blanket and offers me a snack before we get going. I take the blanket, hoping it'll make a temporary substitute for Jaxon, but the rest I decline. I turn my attention back out the window and touch my eyes. They're already puffy.

The pilot's voice comes over the intercom, "Everyone has just about boarded, so we'll close the doors soon and be on our way to Chicago. The flight attendants will provide US customs forms and connecting flight instructions as we get closer to our destination."

I close my eyes, lay my head back, and sigh. Then, I feel someone take the seat beside me. I don't open my eyes until an amber and caramelized vanilla scent reaches my nostrils. My lids fly open and my gaze locks with his warm, intense brown stare.

"What?" I ask. "Why? How?" I'm babbling, and I know it, so I bite my tongue.

34

He's silent.

I inhale through my nose, then say more calmly, "You're not on the right plane. Yours was supposed to leave before mine."

"Yes," he said, "I am on precisely the right plane."

"You're going to Minnesota? Why?"

He chuckles. "Is why really the right question?"

I squint at him in confusion.

"Well, there's a company in Minneapolis that has been working hard to recruit me. I finally accepted their offer for an on-site interview."

"Oh," I say simply, feeling dumbfounded.

"But the real answer as to why should be much more obvious."

My breath hitches, tears threatening again. "Me?"

He slides a hand up my cheek and under my hair. "Yes, *mia cara*. You."

The end.

Thank you for reading.
If you enjoyed Singles Retreat, please consider leaving a review on
Amazon:
amzn.to/ReviewSinglesRetreat
Goodreads:
bit.ly/SinglesRetreatGoodreads
BookBub:
bit.ly/BookBubSinglesRetreat

Join my newsletter for exciting news and offers, giveaways, and
reviews of other romance. You'll also get a 7-chapter preview of
my book coming in February 2020, *An Orchid Falls*:
https://www.subscribepage.com/AnOrchidFallsPreview

Continue reading for the first chapter of *An Orchid Falls*.

An Orchid Falls

Chapter 1

Calli

*T*his is it. Tonight. The. End.

Callista Stockton slid the vodka back into the upper cabinet and flipped off the light switch. With her second martini in hand, she rounded the pristine white marble peninsula and went to the table where, once her eyes adjusted, she would still be able to see the entirety of the freshly remodeled kitchen, as well as the front door. A haunting glow emitted from the only remaining light in the house—an outrageously priced crystal pendant over the sink, the one Bennett had demanded they spend nearly six thousand dollars to have as a centerpiece in the kitchen. Shards of light created tiny rainbows on the far wall, but Calli wondered if there really was anything as bright as a rainbow that could cut through her current darkness.

The second martini had less of a bite than the first, but she still sighed loudly after the first sip, then chewed an olive to chase away the burn. She reached for the pack of Marlboro Lights and tapped it hard several times into her palm. She didn't smoke, at least she hadn't since she found out she was pregnant with her first son seventeen years prior. Her *oh-so-loving* husband, Bennett, had rejoiced when she'd given him the news of the pregnancy, and his first words after swinging her off the ground in a big hug were, *I guess this means you'll give up those nasty cigarettes.* He'd urged her to quit throughout college and into their first year of marriage. She had chalked it up to his love and concern over her, then over the baby. Quitting was tough, but her baby had been the motivation she'd needed.

She pulled the gold tab, feeling a little evil satisfaction and sweet revenge as she slid the first cigarette from the pack. This would eat Bennett alive—not only the fact that she was smoking, but that she dared to do so in his house, in his brand spanking new kitchen. *Strike that, Calli. This house is about to be yours.* She glared at the stack of papers sitting to her right, curved from how they'd been folded and stuffed into the envelope she'd signed for with the postman that afternoon.

As soon as she'd finished reading it the first time, she called Sue to ask if her older son, Jax, could spend the night with his friend. Then she did the same for Kent. Thank God that Jill loved having Kent over to keep Colton entertained—no matter that it was a school night.

It had been two hours since Bennett's plane from Tucson had landed. She'd checked with the airline; the flight had been on time. Since they lived twenty minutes from the airport, he should have been home long ago . . . or at any minute now. Reaching for the lighter, she watched the door and waited, hoping that he'd come in just as she lit the thing. He didn't.

She pressed the button—no roller or actual flame, just a click and a little burning glow. That was one more thing that was no longer the same. Bringing the glow to the end of the cigarette, she pulled the smoke into her mouth as the end sizzled, then inhaled. Immediately, her throat and lungs constricted, spasming against the burning infiltration. Calli coughed, hard. Her eyes watered, but she didn't extinguish the thing. Instead, she stared at the smoke licking from the end, at the paper burning back and creating ash. She smelled the air. That freshly lit smell was already turning into rancid, old-smoke stench. It was gross. She wasn't about to become a smoker again, but she hoped to make a point tonight.

She tried again, taking a small drag on the butt. The taste wasn't any better, so she laid it down in the bowl sitting by her martini glass and smirked at the sight. Bennett's grandmother's fine china bowl with the gold-inlaid ring became her ashtray. He'd just love that part too. Good.

Calli let the cigarette burn to a stump, then stabbed it out and stirred the ashes in hopes that it'd look like she'd actually smoked it. She read through the first paper in the stack again, an unnecessary action as she'd already memorized the important parts and rehearsed what she'd say to her philandering husband. She waited. A fight for the ages was in store for the evening.

An hour and a half later, the security system beeped, announcing that a door had been opened. Calli, still seated at the dining room table, looked up to see Bennett sneaking inside as quietly as possible. He lifted the rolling suitcase and gently placed it beside the front door and hung his shoulder bag over the stair rail, careful not to make much sound. Of course, he thought the house was asleep. It normally would have been at eleven on a weekday.

Calli had lost much of her gusto as her two drinks settled and she had waited. She'd let several more cigarettes burn and had ripped the envelope to shreds. The evidence of her fidgety wait sat in a pile next to the fine china turned ashtray. Mildly, she said, "I expected you'd have been here hours ago."

Despite her resigned and quiet tone, Bennett startled, just about jumping out of his skin. He wore a suit, but the shirt was already half unbuttoned, and the tie hung loose. He stammered, "I...uh..."

Calli held up a hand and rolled her eyes. She didn't want to hear any excuses about how traffic was bad or he got a call from the office or whatever he wanted to make up this time. She would have thought he'd been more practiced at lying to her since he'd been doing it for nearly sixteen years that she could reckon.

She didn't look away from him though. She wanted to see the shock and surprise as he took in the sight of her at the table, the empty martini in hand, the cigarette box and lighter scattered beside the delicate bowl with extinguished butts. In his reaction, he didn't let her down. With every step he took toward the dinette, his jaw dropped a little further open and his hands spread as if to ask, *What the fuck?* Though she wanted to celebrate the fact that she'd stabbed him and drawn a reaction, Calli schooled her expression to neutral and reached for the papers.

"Are you smoking?" Bennett asked. "Where are the boys?"

She ignored his questions. Her voice dry and husky from the smoking attempt, she summarized the key pieces of the summons in her hand: "Wallace County District Court. Jolene Hodge, plaintiff, has filed a claim for child support against Bennett Stockton, defendant."

Bennett shifted out of his cautious approach, rushed to the table, and snatched the papers from Calli's hand. "How dare she?" he said, outraged.

"I presume that means you know this Jolene Hodge person."

"It's impossible that the kid is mine!"

"...and you knew she was pregnant."

"What?" He snapped his head up from the documents. "Oh, no."

Calli didn't try to hide how exasperated she felt as she let out a heavy sigh and shook her head. "I *thought* we were past your affairs. I *thought* you had listened to the therapist. I *thought* we were getting back to being partners in this marriage." She fell back against the chair with her arms crossed. "Obviously, I *thought* wrong."

"No. Cal..." His voice slipped into that soothing tone he'd used on her too many times before. Actually, placating was probably the better description.

His attempt to calm her wasn't going to work now. She simply glared at him. Heedless of everything she thought her look would say to him, he continued. "Jolene is old news. Before we started seeing a therapist."

"Really, Ben? Her name isn't familiar." Calli shook her head. She'd done the math. "The papers say the baby is two months old." She raised a questioning brow at her husband. They had been going to the therapist for nearly eighteen months, and one of the conditions in redeveloping their trust was that everything was put on the table. Clearly, he'd assumed he was exempt from yet another rule.

He said nothing, which, in Calli's mind, only further confirmed his latest lie of omission.

"Listen, Ben. It's over. We are over. You can sleep in the guest room downstairs tonight." She stood. "Tomorrow, you should pack your things and go to your mother's."

"What? No, Cal. I'm not leaving. We're doing good, trying to work things out. For the boys' sakes."

She leaned forward, hands on the table supporting her weight, and looked squarely into his eyes. "Let me make this very clear. Our marriage is over. I can't handle any more affairs." Truly, one was too many, but her mother had always said, *Marriage is tough, it requires work. You have to keep forgiving each other.* Hell, their therapist had said as much. Calli had forgiven Bennett for far too long and for far too many indiscretions. For that matter, how many did she still *not* know about? Their separation had been coming for years. Calli would just have to deal with her mother's judgment over the broken marriage. It wouldn't be the first time she didn't live up to

Isabelle Lindley's expectations. She sighed away the errant thoughts. "Tomorrow, I will find a divorce attorney and file the appropriate papers."

In that instant, his pleading eyes turned hard and all business. He dropped a fist onto the table, causing the bowl to clatter and ashes to spill. "This is my house and my family, and I will fight for what is mine. I am not leaving."

He reached for her, but she backed away. "Very well, then I'll pack myself and the boys and we'll go to Lindleyi Manor to stay with my parents. I'd hoped that you'd make this easy and the boys could finish out high school. But I guess I'll have to enroll them down there."

Bennett kicked a chair out of his way.

Calli jumped.

He yelled, "I said we are going to work this out. I'm not going anywhere, and you are not taking my boys away either."

Prepared for this reaction, Calli nodded and evenly asked, "Are you going to take time off work to see to Kent's special needs at school? Or make sure that he takes his meds every day? Or to make sure he gets to the psychologist for his appointments? You're gone before he even wakes up and half the time, you're gone when he goes to bed. Are you going to sacrifice your business travel or time at your *precious office* in favor of your kids?"

Bennett remained quiet.

"I didn't think so." She stood a bit taller. Her voice was firm and final when she continued, "One way or another, I won't be staying here with you. I am the boys' caretaker, and if you won't leave, we must." After a moment, she softened. "Ben, it'll be easiest if you go to your mother's while we figure out our next steps."

"Cal, we can't just call it quits, we have twenty-one years invested." He reached out again.

She'd said her piece and silently picked up the glass and walked around the peninsula to the sink. She was done giving into his reasons and logic. They all made sense for him, but not for her.

"Calli!" Quite mercurial, his volume rose a notch. "This is ridiculous. I made you. I made this home. I've funded everything from the remodels to the cars to Kent's therapy to the insanity of a marriage counselor. Everything you have is because of me. Where would you be if it wasn't for me?"

She slammed the glass down on the marble counter. "I'd hopefully have a husband who didn't jump into the sack with every piece of ass he could find."

"What did you expect when you shriveled up like a prune after Kent?"

Calli's jaw hung open in silence. She couldn't believe that he'd find a way to make his cheating her fault or that he'd call her something so repulsive.

"Well?"

"Ya know what? Fuck you, Bennett! That's where this all started . . . when you showed me who you *really* and *truly* are. Kent was a hard baby and I had an eighteen-month-old to take care of too. You didn't help out at all, and I was exhausted. Any man worth his salt would have supported his wife."

"You knew when you married me that I had strong sexual needs."

"Yeah, but I didn't think a month off would have caused you to hop in bed with the nearest set of tits on legs."

"It was way more than a month, and you know it!"

"It's not like you tried much once I was back on my feet. It was always my responsibility to initiate sex, and that just got old. Who wants to feel like their partner thinks making love is a chore?" She'd tried several more times over the years to break the frigid gap between them. He'd gone through the motions, but they never really connected again as they had before Kent. She hadn't known why at the time, and she had blamed herself. Years had passed before she finally pieced together his patterns, and when she did recognize the signs, she knew exactly when it had all started.

Bennett started to say something else, but Calli took in a deep breath and released a long cleansing exhale. Holding up a hand, she said, "Listen, that's all in the past. We are where we are because we haven't really been a couple since Kent was born. We tried. Give us a fucking E for effort, but I just can't anymore. It's time to move on. I'll have the papers delivered to your office. What's your new secretary's name? I'll call her and have her watch for them."

Bennett's face turned bright red . . . so much so that it glowed even in the dim light. His eyes shifted down and away as he quietly said, "Zoe."

Calli stared at his reaction for a minute, a reaction that could only mean one thing. Her jaw fell and her brows rose in astonished disgust. Her hands flew in wild gesticulation as she launched into a full-on tirade. "Un-fucking-believable. You're fucking her! That's where you were tonight, why you're late. You ran right over to your newest little mistress to get your rocks off before you had to come home to the old ball and chain. You are fucking disgusting, do you know that? And you know what else? I have never once cheated on you, though I've had good reason to. It's been years since I've had sex, and you were off banging some ho-bag. Do you even care a little about my feelings anymore? Just a stitch?"

"No. I don't." Bennett ran a hand over his thinning hair and went to the basement door. With his hand on the knob, poised to go downstairs, he looked back and said, "There. Are you fucking happy? I've admitted it."

An Orchid Falls will be available for purchase at your favorite online retailer on February 1, 2020.
This link will take you to a page that links to all the online bookstores:
bit.ly/OrderAnOrchidFalls

Preorder yours today!
Or . . .
Join my newsletter for exciting news and offers, giveaways, and reviews of other romance. You'll also get a 7 chapter preview of my book coming in February 2020, *An Orchid Falls:*
https://www.subscribepage.com/AnOrchidFallsPreview

About the Author

Julia O. Greene is a pen name for Susan Stradiotto who is typically a fantasy and speculative fiction author. As the material she writes doesn't serve the romance audience, she decided to pay tribute to her grandmother in her contemporary fiction. Susan lives in Eden Prairie, Minnesota with her husband, three children, and a crazy Bernese Mountain Dog named Delaunay. Stories of all kinds are her passion, and she has always been a voracious reader, lover of worlds, and hoarder of books. Her infatuation with well-developed characters sometimes rivals relationships with real people.

Book reviews are the best way to support an author!

If you enjoyed this story, please leave a review on Amazon, Goodreads, BookBub, Facebook, or any other place you can give a shout out!

www.ingramcontent.com/pod-product-compliance
Lightning Source LLC
Chambersburg PA
CBHW070651130626
46555CB00006B/2824